The Magic Kingdom

STORYBOOK

Written and Illustrated by Jason Grandt

DISNEY PRESS

New York • Los Angeles

For information address Disney Press,
1101 Flower Street, Glendale, California 91201
Editor: Jessica Ward
Designer: Stef Lum

This author would like to thank all the Walt Disney Imagineers,
animators, and artists both past and present whose inspiration and
guidance can be found throughout these pages; my family and
friends for all their support and encouragement; my editor, Jessie,
for her creative partnership and extreme patience in the creation
of this book; and Alex, Jason, and Scott for making it look so easy.

ISBN 978-1-4231-1973-9

First Edition
10 9 8 7 6 5 4 3 2 1
F850-6835-5-13261
Printed in Singapore

for **BRENNAN**

Here you leave today
and enter the world
of Yesterday, Tomorrow
and Fantasy

CONTENTS

MAIN STREET, U.S.A.

A CAREFREE PLACE FROM TIMES PAST...

A HOME ON MAIN STREET

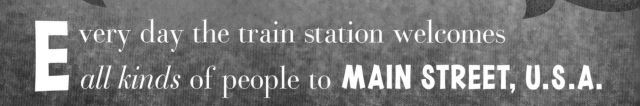

Every day the train station welcomes *all kinds* of people to **MAIN STREET, U.S.A.**

Some are here to **WORK**...

Some are here to **SHOP**...

Some are here to **PLAY**...

However, today someone got off the train
with nowhere to go. A little pup was
looking for **A PLACE TO CALL HOME.**

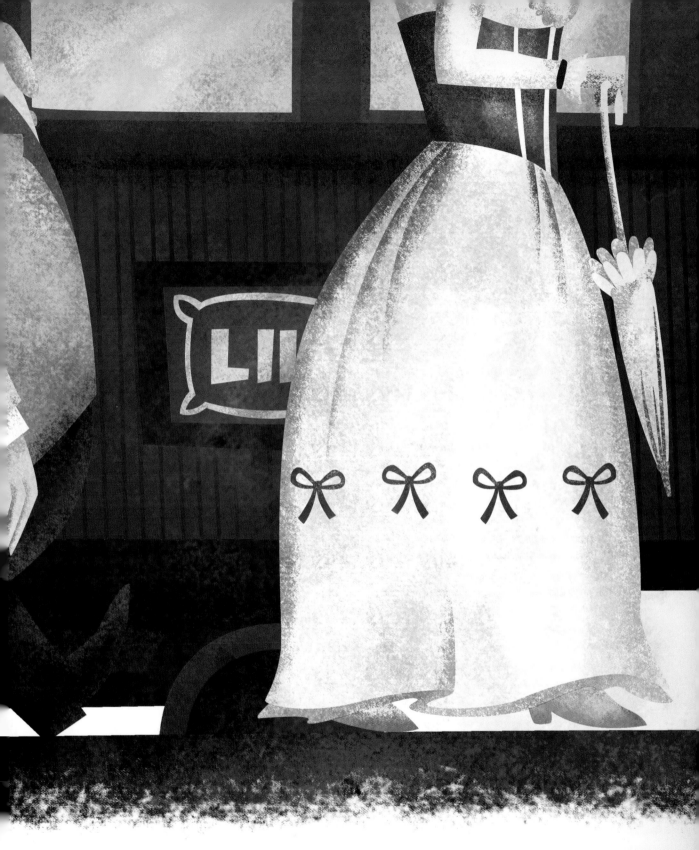

Surely, somewhere on Main Street

FIT THE BILL.

His first stop was the
Main Street **BARBER SHOP.**

Although the barber *loved* dogs, he said
he didn't have the time to clean up fur too.

The Crystal Arts shop was next,
and it was *breathtaking*.

Everything was so **SHINY, SO BEAUTIFUL,** and

The shopkeeper *barely* got the little pup out before he broke everything with his TAIL.

The Main Street Bakery might
make a **GOOD HOME.**

It *looked* delicious.

It *smelled* delicious.

And it *tasted* delicious!

It's a good thing dogs can eat on the run,
because the pup was out the door
before he knew it!

Even the ice cream parlor gave the
pup the **SCOOP OUT THE DOOR.**

The little pup was feeling down on his luck as he crossed Center Street. But then he found someone else that seemed to be *worse off* than he was.

"I've lost my cat," the little girl said, "and I can't find her." The little pup felt so sorry for the girl that **HE DECIDED TO HELP.**

He put his nose into action and
sniffed up one side of Main Street
and then down the other.

But *still* no sign of that cat.

All the little pup could
smell was HOT POPCORN.

POP! POP! MEOW!

Pop, pop, meow? There by the popcorn
wagon was the little girl's cat up in a tree!

The little dog
started to bark,
and before
he knew it,
the little girl
was there
and a fire truck
was *on its way.*

As one fireman handed the cat down
to the thankful girl, the fire chief picked
up the little pup. "So my little hero,
what's your name?" he asked.

"*What*? No name tag?
No place to go home to?
How'd you like to come live
with us at the fire station?"

The pup gave the fire chief a BIG KISS.

The days of looking for a home were now over
for the little pup. He had a place to sleep, plenty
of food to eat, and, *most importantly,*
PEOPLE WHO LOVED HIM.

MAIN STREET

7 THE END 1

FIRE DEPT.

**THE WONDER WORLD OF
NATURE'S OWN REALM . . .**

DONALD'S WILD BIRD CHASE

Ace photographer Donald Duck walked
through the jungle. *Rare Birds* magazine
had sent him on a **SPECIAL EXPEDITION.**

Donald's mission was to find and photograph
the rare and mischievous ARACUAN BIRD...
the clown of the jungle.

Donald set off on his jungle cruise.
He wondered what *dangers* and *mysteries*
awaited him around each bend in the **RIVER.**

Donald saw many kinds of
CREATURES in the jungle.

Some *flew,*

some *ran,*

and some *swam.*

Some were very FRIENDLY...

... and some were very HUNGRY, but very
few were both. *None* of them knew
where the Aracuan bird was.

It was easier to search lower . . .
but *sometimes* safer to search **HIGHER!**

Donald searched *here,*

there,

everywhere!

41

Donald even asked the hyenas,
but they were **LAUGHING** too hard to answer.

"*Hey*, what's so funny?
Have you seen him or not?"

The **ANCIENT TEMPLE** was Donald's
next stop on the river.

Donald knew he was getting close.
The writing was on the walls.

SUDDENLY, Donald saw him —

THE ARACUAN!!!

The Aracuan took off down the river.
Nothing could stop Donald now!

Not **PIRANHAS,**

not **CROCODILES,**

not *even* a . . .

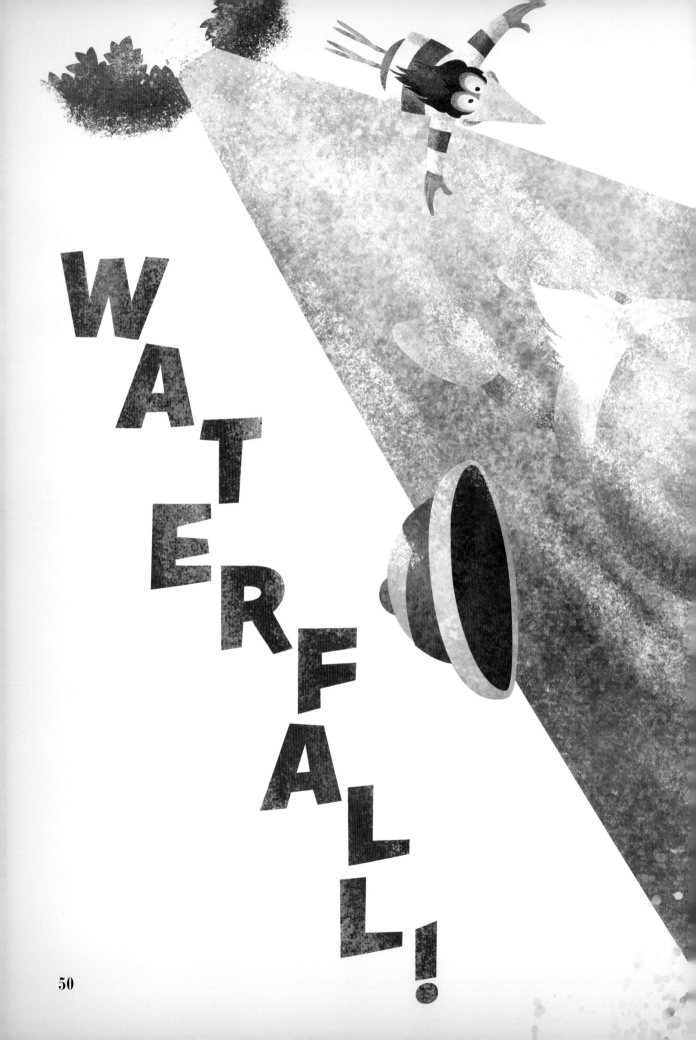

WATERFALL!

SPLAT!

Donald landed
on the rocks below,
and his camera
went **FLYING.**

SNAP!

Luckily, the camera didn't get ruined.
Donald got the photo — and the **COVER STORY!**

FANTASYLAND

THE HAPPIEST KINGDOM
OF THEM ALL . . .

THE MADDEST TEA PARTY

It's another merry unbirthday in Wonderland. The March Hare and the Mad Hatter were ready to start the party when a *small problem* arose: **SMALL TEACUPS.**

"Wouldn't it be grand to have a *bigger* cup of tea?" asked the March Hare.

"Indeed! It is your unbirthday. You should have the **BIGGEST CUP** of all!" replied the Mad Hatter.

"Oh, yes, the *bigger*, **THE GRANDER!**" said the Hare. "Well then, maybe this will help," proclaimed his silly friend, holding a small teapot.

The cup of tea was poured and the two drank away.
"This cup *still* seems pretty small to me…"

"But now I seem *pretty* small compared to it!" said the March Hare as the two were swallowed by the **GIANT TEACUP.**

"Yes, we are quite small, aren't we? But something else seems **STRANGE** ... Are we moving about in this rather *large* teacup?"

"I dare say we are.
But not just moving,
SPINNING!!!"

"Oh, dear, I believe
we are spinning!
Spin, spin, **SPINNING!!!**"

And *spin* the duo did.
From teapot to teapot they twirled
around the table . . .

whirling and *whirling* faster and faster
and faster **STILL.**

Near the edge and back again,
from the sugar to the saucer . . .

. . . from the biscuits to the jam.
Wilder and *wilder* and **WILDER!**

Then it **STOPPED.**

"I'll say, I'm sure glad *that* is over,"
said the Mad Hatter.

"*Indeed,*" said the March Hare, "it's much too
hard to drink tea when one is spinning
about in a teacup."

"Of course, you could spin some more. **A LOT** more . . ."

"Who said that?" asked the pair.

"Oh, I guess, I guess *that* would be **ME!**"

"Well sir, I think we're done spinning, thank you," said the March Hare.

"Yes indeed, *done and done*," followed the Mad Hatter.

"But I haven't twirled you *here*,
whirled you *there* or *there*,
and spun you back here again.
What a shame," said the CHESHIRE CAT.

"Well, if we're going to spin some more, I'd *love* to have a biscuit first," said the March Hare, knowing that eating a biscuit would return them to their **NORMAL SIZE.**

"*A biscuit?*" asked the Cheshire Cat.

"Oh, *yes*, a **BISCUIT AND ... JAM!**" exclaimed the Mad Hatter as he jumped out of the cup. He landed on the end of a *spoon*, flinging jam into the Cheshire Cat's face. The March Hare grabbed a biscuit for the two to eat.

As quickly as they had *shrunk*, the Mad Hatter and the March Hare grew back to their **FULL SIZE.**

They were ready to turn the tables on the Cheshire Cat when he suddenly began to *vanish*.

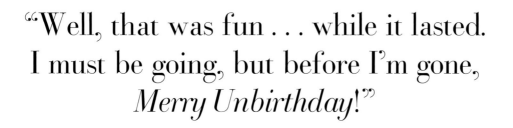

"Well, that was fun . . . while it lasted.
I must be going, but before I'm gone,
Merry Unbirthday!"

"Oh, yes, **MERRY UNBIRTHDAY,**"
said the Mad Hatter.

"Wait, it's *my* unbirthday, too,"
said the March Hare.

"Well then . . ."

"a *very* Merry
Unbirthday
to you!"

"To **ME?**"
"To **YOU!**"

FRONTIERLAND

TALL TALES AND TRUE
FROM THE LEGENDARY PAST...

It was a sunny day in the **BRIAR PATCH,** but not everyone was feeling satisfactual. "Brer Bunnie, you *ready* to go fishin'?" asked Brer Papa.

"I dunno, I GUESS . . ."

"Son, looks like you got a case of the **BRIAR BLUES,** and there's only one remedy for that. You *gotta* find your laughin' place."

"You see once Brer Turtle
had a *bad* case of the blues
ruinin' his day . . ."

"He was out sunnin'
on the riverbank
mindin' his
own business . . ."

"... when a bunch of youngins skipped a stone
through the mud and got his shell all dirty.
He was *mighty* **VEXED**..."

"So he went lookin' for a place to clean himself and found the **RAINBOW CAVERNS.**"

"*Splishin'* and *splashin'* away, he knew
he had found his laughin' place!"

"Is that why all the turtles go there to play?"
asked Brer Bunnie.

"YOU BET!"

"**BRER SKUNK** had the blues once, too. Critters kept tellin' him he *smelled rotten*, so he went searchin' for the best smellin' place he could find."

"The **FLOWER PATCH!**
Now all the animals think he smells great!
And you know *what*? He does!"

"Even I had the blues once,
REAL BAD..."

"Really?" asked Brer Bunnie.

"Oh, *sure*,
I had gone left the briar patch
to get things right again."

"Only problem was that Brer Fox
and Brer Bear were *hot* on my tail,
tryin' to cause me **TROUBLE.**"

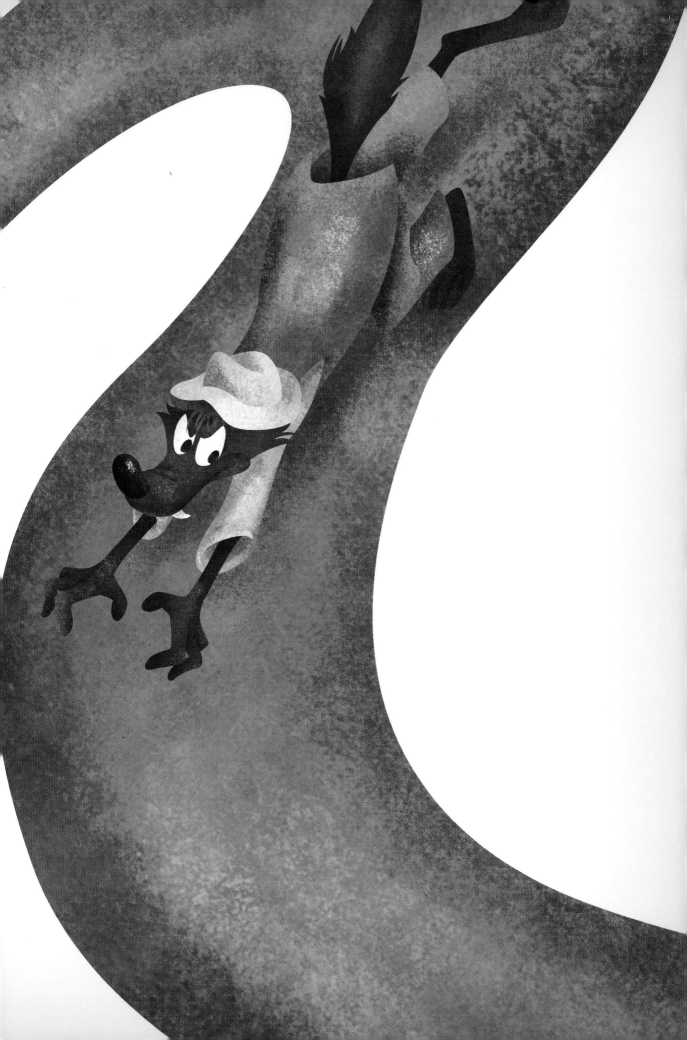

"It looked like Brer Fox
had me
DONE FOR GOOD…"

"... but I **ESCAPED!**"

"I *jumped* down Chickapin Hill,
back into the briar patch.
Brer Fox had done the same ..."

"... but sure *wished* he hadn't!"

100

"I never laughed so hard in my life! Next thing I know, my blues is *gone*. **LONG GONE.**"

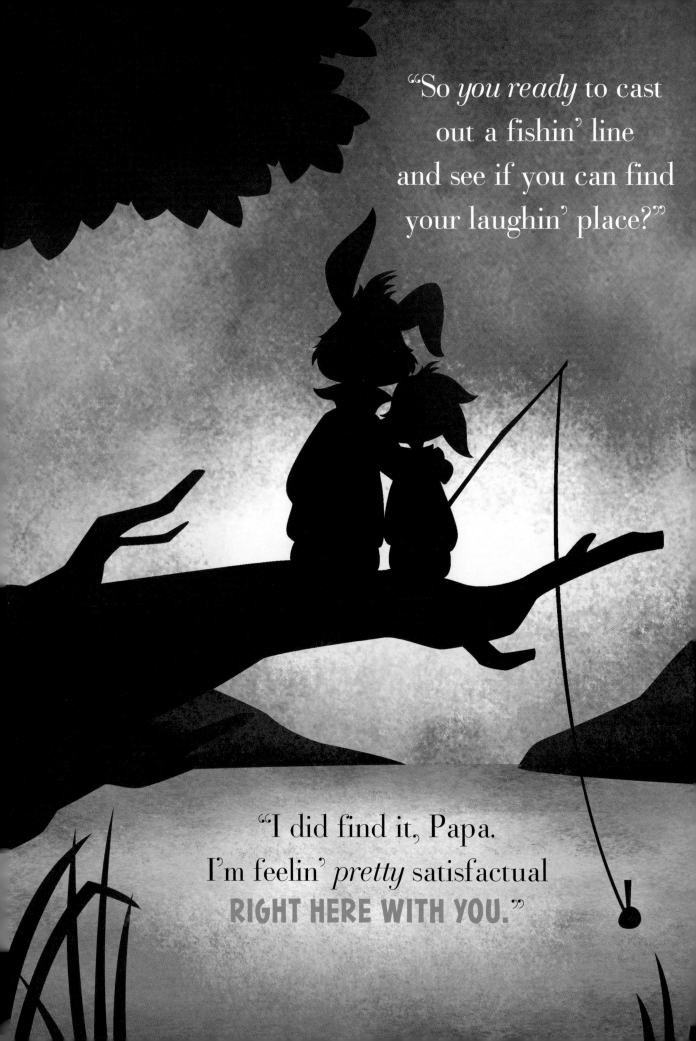

"So *you ready* to cast
out a fishin' line
and see if you can find
your laughin' place?"

"I did find it, Papa.
I'm feelin' *pretty* satisfactual
RIGHT HERE WITH YOU."

PROMISE OF THINGS
TO COME . . .

PLUTO'S

MISSION TO SPACE

The cookies were fresh out of the oven, and Minnie had made Mickey's favorite: **GINGERBREAD ROBOTS!**

Mickey was working in outer space,
so the cookies would be sent in the space-mail.
PLUTO was on his way to the spaceport
when he ran into a *small problem.*

Actually, it was two small problems!

Two **MARTIAN CHIPMUNKS**
named Chip 'n' Dale
snatched Mickey's cookies!

Pluto took off and *chased* them
down the street, into the PeopleMover,
and into SPACE MOUNTAIN.

He thought he had them, but the two
alien rascals *hopped* into a ROCKET SHIP.

Pluto was barely able to grab on
as the ship began to move, and he held
on tight as they *zipped* through the
ENERGIZER TUBE.

3... 2... 1..

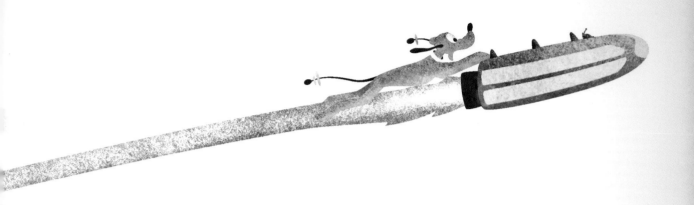

BLAST OFF!!!!

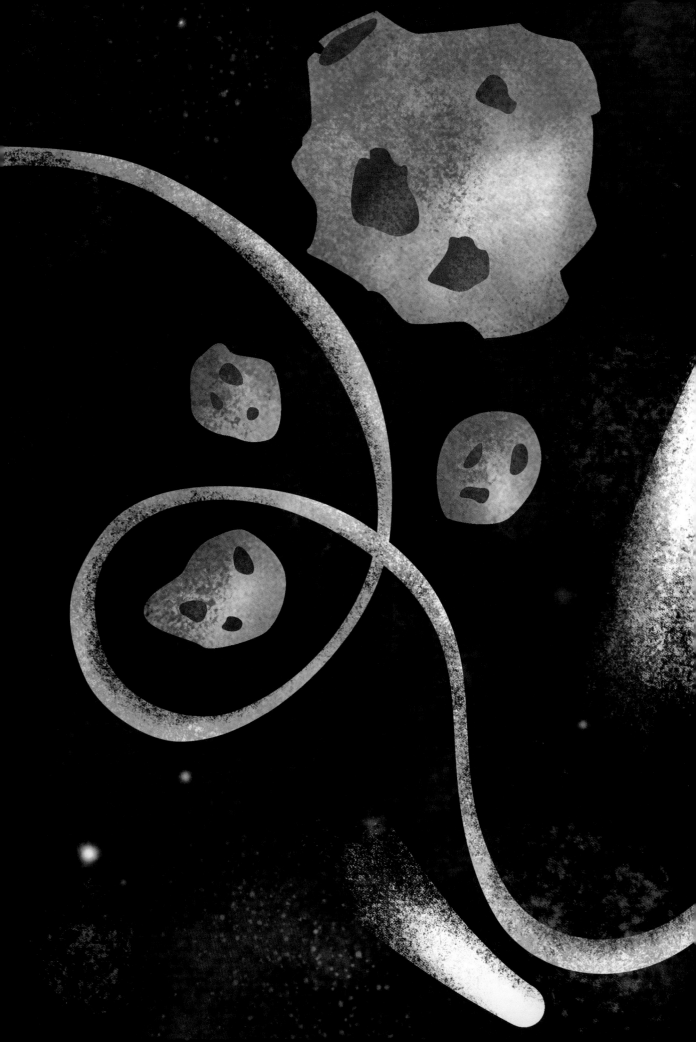

The chipmunks tried to get Pluto
to let go by *flying* through
asteroid fields, chasing COMETS.

dipping into **BLACK HOLES,**

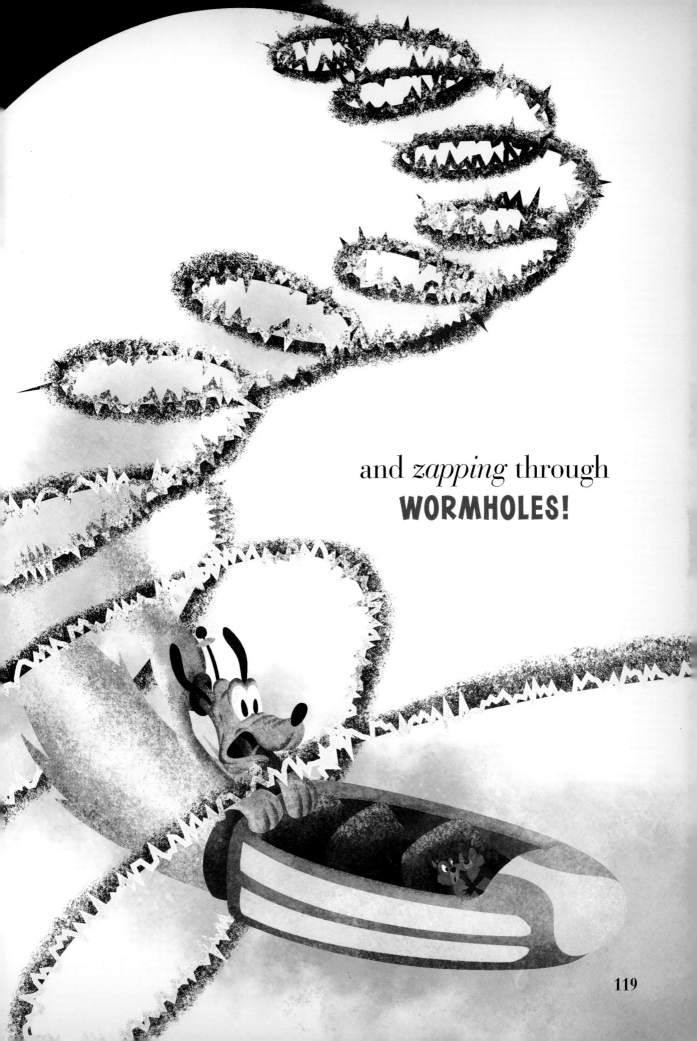

and *zapping* through
WORMHOLES!

119

Fortunately,
the chipmunks became
distracted by an
ACORN SUPERNOVA,
and Pluto took his chance.
He climbed aboard and
grabbed the controls.
Unfortunately, dogs
really don't fly
rocket ships very well.

The ship **BLASTED** into
the arrivals port of
Mickey's space station and
sent the three *flying*
through the air.

Passengers on recent space flights got an
unexpected **SURPRISE** with their luggage:

a few four-legged creatures mixed in with their
clothes . . . and some *really* tasty cookies!

Everyone got an unexpected surprise.
Mickey got to see his pup, Pluto, and
Chip 'n' Dale got one-way tickets
HOME TO MARS!